I read this book all by myself

For Louie Jarman, who makes delicious chocolate cakes and
Josh Pearce who likes eating them – JJ
For Davide, the magic kid – AG

A Red Fox Book

Published by Random House Children's Books
61-63 Uxbridge Road, London W5 5SA

A division of the Random House Group Ltd
London Melbourne Sydney Auckland
Johannesburg and agencies throughout the world

5 7 9 10 8 6 4

First published in Great Britain by Red Fox 2001

Published in hardback by Heinemann Library, a division of
Reed Educational and Professional Publishing Limited,
by arrangement with Random House Children's Books

Printed in Singapore by Tien Wah Press

THE RANDOM HOUSE GROUP Limited Reg. No. 954009
www.kidsatrandomhouse.co.uk

ISBN 0 09 941734 0 (paperback)
ISBN 0 431 02410 3 (hardback)

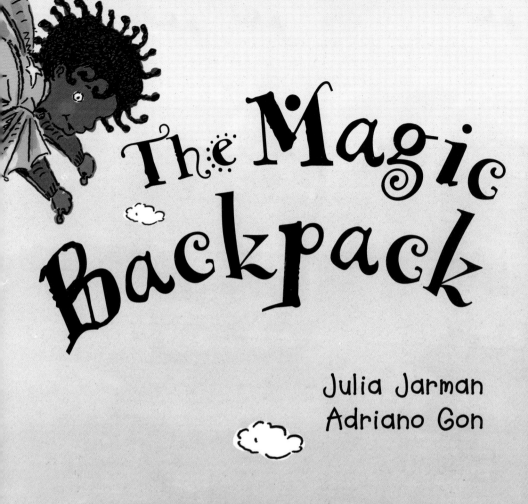

The Magic Backpack

Julia Jarman
Adriano Gon

RED FOX

Josh was having a forgetful week.
On Monday he forgot his reading book.

On Tuesday he forgot his PE kit.

On Wednesday he forgot it
was a school day and he
was very nearly late.

Then he remembered
his magic backpack.

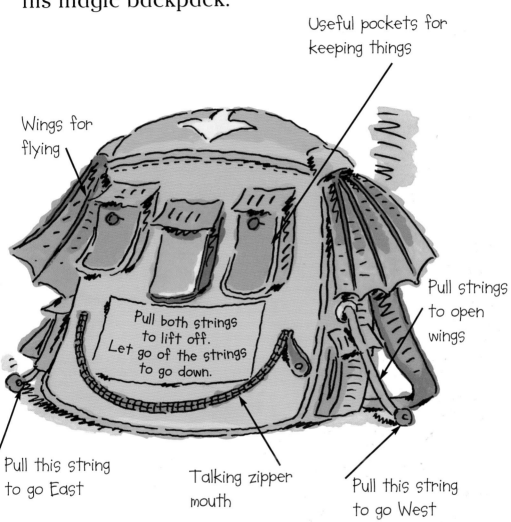

Useful pockets for
keeping things

Wings for
flying

Pull both strings
to lift off.
Let go of the strings
to go down.

Pull strings
to open
wings

Pull this string
to go East

Talking zipper
mouth

Pull this string
to go West

Josh's magic backpack was very useful.
It had amazing powers.

Josh pulled the strings of his magic backpack and . . .

If I'm late, Mrs Crumble will grumble!

Vroosh!

. . . he got to school just in time.

Mrs Crumble said, "Sit down quickly, Josh. We are looking at this recipe and this map of the world. Today we will find out where the ingredients – the things we will need to make our cake – come from."

CHOCOLATE CAKE
INGREDIENTS
170 g. self-raising flour
170 g. soft butter
170 g. caster sugar   3 eggs
1 level teaspoon of baking powder
3 level tablespoons of <u>cocoa</u> powder
4 tablespoons of warm water

"Tomorrow we shall make a delicious chocolate cake."

"Eggs come from hens," said Freddie, who lived on a farm.

"You can bring the eggs," said Mrs Crumble.

"Butter comes from cows' milk," said Katie.

"Flour comes from wheat," said Melanie.

"Sugar comes from sugar cane,"
said Nadia.

"Or sugar beet," said James.

Some sugar cane grows in Mauritius.

Some sugar beet grows in England.

"Chocolate comes from cocoa," said Tracy.

"My Uncle William has a cocoa plantation in Ghana," said Josh.

"Ghana is in Africa," said Mrs Crumble.

"You can bring the cocoa, Josh, and the chocolate for the delicious chocolate topping. Please, please don't forget."

At home-time, Mrs Crumble gave them all letters. Josh's letter said:

Rustling Firs
Primary School
Kings Road
Ampthill
MK 45 1JP

3 September 2001

Dear Parent,

We are making a chocolate cake on Thursday. Please would you give your son/daughter the following ingredients:

3 level tablespoons of cocoa
100 grams of dark chocolate

Thank you!

Yours sincerely,

Mrs. Crumble

Josh gave Freddie a lift home on his
magic backpack.

They saw a cow being milked and a hen
laying an egg.

When Josh got home, he
told his mum all about
Freddie's farm, but he
forgot to tell her about
the chocolate cake.

On Thursday, Josh flew to school.

Mrs Crumble said, "Did you remember the ingredients, children?"

Freddie had the eggs.

Katie had the butter.

Melanie had the flour.

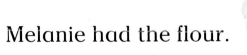

James had the sugar, but Josh had forgotten the cocoa and the chocolate for the delicious chocolate topping.

Everyone was cross with Josh – except Tracy.

It was a mistake!

Mrs Crumble grumbled, "After play we will make a cake, but it won't be a chocolate cake."

Josh had to stay in at playtime. Poor Josh. He was cross with himself. "Why? Why am I so forgetful?" he said aloud. Then he heard a voice:

Josh! Josh! Don't delay! Pull on my strings to save the day!

It was his magic backpack. He had forgotten about that, too. Josh pulled the strings.

ooosh!

His feet left
the ground.

He flew through
the window into
the playground.
"Wait for me!"
said Tracy,
grabbing
his legs.

Josh thought he was going home, or to
the shop, but they flew over his house,
and over the shop. They left the village
behind them and the nearby town.

Suddenly they were flying over the sea!
Josh had never flown so far – or so fast.

"Where are we going?" gasped Tracy.

"To Africa, I think."

"But that's thousands of miles. It will take
hours," said Tracy.

"I hope not," said Josh.

They whizzed over France and Spain, and
over the Mediterranean Sea.

"We're over Africa now!" said Tracy.
"There's desert below."

"And rainforest ahead," said Josh.

He saw a cocoa plantation and let go of
the magic backpack strings.

"Hello, Josh!" said Uncle William.

"Hello, Uncle William," said Josh.
"I need some cocoa and some
chocolate, please."

Goodness me,
it's Josh!

"We're making a cake at school," explained Tracy, "and we've got to get back before playtime ends."

Uncle William laughed.
He thought they were joking.
"Well, there are the cocoa
trees," he said, pointing to
some tall trees.

"See the cocoa beans in the big red and yellow pods. See them drying in the sun."

Tracy tugged Josh's arm.
"Josh, we've got to get back
to bake the cake."

Uncle William laughed again and drove
them to the cocoa factory.

When they got to the factory there were thousands of chocolate bars, and piles of cocoa. Uncle William filled the backpack with cocoa and chocolate bars. "Now you can bake that delicious chocolate cake," he said.

"Thank you!" said Josh. He pulled hard on the strings of his magic backpack and . . .

Vroosh!

. . . they were flying again.

"Goodbye!" called Josh.

They flew back to school . . .

. . . and arrived just as playtime was ending. "Where have you two been?" asked Mrs Crumble.

Here's the cocoa!

"To get the cocoa," said Josh.
"And the chocolate," said Tracy.
They didn't say they had been to Africa.
She wouldn't have believed them.

Everyone helped to make the cake. They mixed butter and sugar and eggs and flour and cocoa. Then they put it in the oven.

While it baked, they melted the chocolate.
Then they mixed it with butter and icing
sugar to make the delicious topping.

When the cake was ready, they iced it and piled it high with chocolate flakes. Their Super-Duper Round the World Chocolate Cake was delicious!

Super-Duper
Round the World Chocolate Cake Recipe

When you see this sign, get an adult to help you.

To make the CAKE

You will need:
170g self-raising flour
170g soft butter
170g caster sugar
1 level teaspoon of baking powder
3 eggs
3 level tablespoons cocoa powder
4 tablespoons of warm water

1. Sift the flour and baking powder into a bowl.

2. Add the butter, sugar and eggs.

4. Beat the mixture with a wooden spoon for a few minutes, then with an electric mixer for one minute.

3. Blend the cocoa powder with the warm water. Add to the bowl.

5. Pre-heat the oven to gas mark 3 or 160°C.

6. Pour the mixture into a cake tin and bake for 40-45 minutes.

44

To make the
TOPPING
You will need:
240g icing sugar
100g dark chocolate
30g butter
3 tablespoons hot
water
chocolate flakes

1. Put the dark chocolate and butter in a bowl.

3. Gradually beat in the icing sugar and water till it is shiny.

2. Melt them by standing the bowl in a pan of hot water.

4. Spread the topping over the cake and decorate with chocolate flakes.

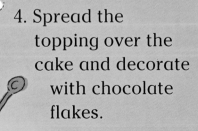

Julia Jarman

Where did you get the idea for this story? I know a little boy called Josh, whose grandparents come from West Africa. He has got a backpack and one day I wondered – what if it were magic?

If you had a magic backpack like Josh, where would you go? I would go to Africa!

What is your favourite food? I'm tempted to say chocolate because I like it so much, but I love food of all sorts. And I love trying new things!

How long did it take to write this story? It's hard to say exactly how long it took to write this story, because I thought of the idea and wrote a bit, and then got stuck, and then wrote a bit more, and so on. Then I sent it to an editor who said, "I like it but . . ." She suggested some changes, so I wrote it again!

Can I be a writer like you? Yes, you can! I have a Writing Recipe for cooking up stories. You can try it too. Find it on my website at www.juliajarman.com.

Adriano Gon

What did you use to paint the pictures in this book? I used wall paint on film. First, I drew the black outlines on the film. Then I added the colours on the back side of the film. You can try it, too.

What would you do if you had a magic backpack? I would go wandering about to all kinds of places, like Josh, until supper.

Where do you live? I live in Trieste on the east side of Italy, very close to Venice and by the Slovenian and Croatian border.

What's your favourite food? I like Chinese, Indian, and Italian food. I love to cook. My specialty is homemade green tagliatelle in spicy clam sauce. I really like to eat with all my friends, round a big table.

What's your favourite place to draw? The bathtub.

What did you like to do when you were a child? What did you hate most? I liked to draw people from my village and roller-skate. I hated doctors and injections.

Will you try and write or draw a story too?

Let your ideas take flight with
Flying Foxes

All the Little Ones – and a Half
by Mary Murphy

Sherman Swaps Shells
by Jane Clarke and Ant Parker

Digging for Dinosaurs
by Judy Waite and Garry Parsons

Shadowhog
by Sandra Ann Horn and Mary McQuillan

The Magic Backpack
by Julia Jarman and Adriano Gon

Jake and the Red Bird
by Ragnhild Scamell and Valeria Petrone